WILLY BEAR

By Mildred Kantrowitz

Illustrated by Nancy Winslow Parker

PARENTS' MAGAZINE PRESS • NEW YORK

24082

Text copyright © 1976 by Mildred Kantrowitz
Illustrations copyright © 1976 by Nancy Winslow Parker
All rights reserved   Printed in the United States of America

Library of Congress Cataloging in Publication Data

Kantrowitz, Mildred.
  Willy Bear,
  SUMMARY: On the eve of his first day at
school, a child projects some of his uneasiness onto
his teddy bear, Willy.
  [1. School stories.   2. Night-Fiction]
I. Parker, Nancy Winslow.   II. Title.
PZ7.K1285Wi   [E]   76-2744
ISBN 0-8193-0883-8   ISBN 0-8193-0884-6 lib. bdg.

To Beginnings

Good-night, Willy.
Close your eyes and go right to sleep.
I kiss you on the tip of your nose.
Just like always.
And when you get up in the morning
I want you to be bright and cheerful,
not cranky. Do you know why?

Tomorrow you are going to school.

School is a very nice place to go.
You have to be big enough, and old enough,
and grown up enough. Just like you.

Now I will kiss you on your toes
and on your ears.
Good-night, Willy Bear.

Willy?
Are you sleeping?
Are you still awake?
Is it too dark in the room?

Now that you
are all grown up
I put out the lights.

I know you're not afraid of the dark!
But would one small light make you feel better?
O.K. Just tonight. There ...
I feel better too.

Good-night, Willy Bear.

Willy?
Are you still awake?
I can see from my bed that your eyes are wide open.
Why can't you fall asleep?
I know the reason. You're thirsty!
Sometimes when you're very thirsty you can't go to sleep.
I will get you a glass of water.

Now drink it slowly.
May I have some?

M-m-m . . . I was thirsty, too.
I feel much better. Don't you?

Good-night, Willy Bear.

Willy?
You're not still awake, are you?
I know what the problem is.

I think that you would like to come over
and snuggle next to me on my soft pillow,
like we always did.
Just because you're all grown up
doesn't mean you can't snuggle anymore.
We're still friends, aren't we?

You feel so nice and soft.

Good-night, Willy Bear.

Willy...?   Where are you!

Oh, there you are. On the floor.
Have you brushed your teeth?
Did you wash your face?
Have you eaten your breakfast?
YOU'RE NOT EVEN DRESSED YET!
Well, I will just have to leave without you.

Oh, Willy Bear, don't look so sad. I still love you.
I always will. If you really want to know,
I'm doing all this just for you. I will go to school first,

and I will meet YOUR new teacher.
I will taste YOUR milk and cookies,
and I will meet YOUR new friends.

Then I will come right home, and
I'll tell you all about it.
Now you sit here at the window where
you can watch me leave. I will wave.
You're very brave, Willy.
You are all grown up!

Good-bye, Willy Bear.

After working as an interior display designer, then moving on to book design and her present job as art director of a publishing house, MILDRED KANTROWITZ decided she might like to write her own children's books. That was five years—and five tales—ago. Her first picture book for Parents' Magazine Press, Maxie, *was selected as one of the best books of the year 1970. Her subsequent stories—*I Wonder if Herbie's Home Yet, Goodbye, Kitchen, *and* When Violet Died *have all received critical acclaim. The mother of two daughters, the author lives in New York City.*

NANCY WINSLOW PARKER, a former art director and designer herself, has illustrated six books, one of them a Junior Literary Guild selection. She studied at Mills College in California and at the Art Students League and the School of Visual Arts in New York. Willy Bear *is the second book she has illustrated for Parents' Magazine Press, following* The Goat in the Rug. *Ms. Parker lives in New York City and spends summers on the Jersey Shore with her two woolly bichons frises.*